RIDE, ROLL, RUN

TIME FOR FUN!

Written by
VALERIE BOLLING

Illustrated by
SABRENA KHADIJA

School's done!

Ride, roll, run.

Step, push.
Glide, whoosh!

Stand tall.

Don't fall!

Speed, cruise.

Cool views!

Pedal, pump.
Speed bump!

Reach, swing.
Hold, cling.

Almost there . . .
Do you dare?

Blank sidewalk.
Draw with chalk.

Flowers, birds.
Wondrous words.

Slide, duck.
Don't get struck!

Throw, catch.
Win match!

Throw a stone.
Hop in zone.
Up, down.
Touch ground.

Dribble, fake.
Fast break!

Shoot, wish.
Swoop, swish!

Tap, rebound.
Pass around.

Watch it soar.

SCORE!

Turn slow . . .
Then GO!

Jump, twirl.
Spin, whirl.

Walk the line.

Count to ten.
Do it again.

Scatter, chase.
Touch base!

Clap, clang.
Bam, bang!
Boom, bop.
Rhythms drop!

Splish, splash!
Drenched fast.

Cold spray.
Hooray!

Ride, roll, run.

Friends and fun!

For Isaiah, Normani, Arthur, Emma, Holly,
and all the children who love to have fun in the city,
the suburbs, and the country—wherever they may be
—V.B.

To my family who are also my friends, and my little nephews
who I hope grow up having as much fun as we did
—S.K.

The artwork for this book was created digitally.

Library of Congress Control Number 2021947703
ISBN 978-1-4197-5629-0

Text © 2022 Valerie Bolling
Illustrations © 2022 Sabrena Khadija
Book design by Heather Kelly

Published in 2022 by Abrams Appleseed, an imprint of ABRAMS.

Printed and bound in China
10 9 8 7 6 5 4 3 2 1

For bulk discount inquiries,
contact specialsales@abramsbooks.com.

ABRAMS The Art of Books
195 Broadway, New York, NY 10007
abramsbooks.com